Ernie
the Blue Beagle

Sarah Tooker
Sylvia Thomson

illustrations by Rodney Cooke

This book is dedicated to Ernie, my beloved Blue Bilingual Beagle
who will always hold a very special place in my heart.

Te amo, Ernesto. Run free, until we meet again!

I am blue.

It's *not* because I'm sad. I did *not* fall into a bucket of blue paint and I did *not* eat too many blueberries.
I was born this way.

I am a Blue Beagle. One in a million, one of a kind, true blue dog!

But that's not the *only* thing that makes me special...

I live in a park with many other dogs.

We are all waiting for the day when we are chosen to be someone's best friend. Everyday humans come to visit and sometimes they pick one of us to take home with them.

Someday I will be chosen by a family and I will be the best dog-friend ever! I will do tricks for them and they will feed me and give me a cozy bed of my own.

They will be my forever-family and I will be their true Blue Beagle!

Today is the day.
My forever-family is on their way!

I'm jumping and bouncing up and down
happily spinning round and round!

Walk? Yes, I love to walk!
But watch me run and jump and...*FLOP!*

SPLOOSH!
Ta da!!! I *love* puddles!

The big man with the fuzzy face is talking to the family.
I think he's telling them all about me!

"He's a noisy pup,
A messy pup,
A clumsy pup too.
He's a smelly pup,
A silly pup,
And the color blue!
Maybe he's *not* the dog for you."

Me? Messy?
Wait, don't go away. Not yet!

Give me a bath and you will see,
I'm the perfect Blue Beagle for your family!

Today is my lucky day.
Things are going my way!

The next family that comes through the gate
will surely think that I am great!

I will show them my Blue Beagle tricks.
I'll sing loudly and dance a jiggity-jig!

Just as I'm getting jiggy,
I snort like a pot-belly piggy!

"SNORT...SNORT...SNORT!"

I can't help it, you see...
It just comes out of me.

The big man with the fuzzy face is talking to the lady.
He must be telling her all about me!

"He's a noisy pup,
A messy pup,
A clumsy pup too.
He's a smelly pup,
A silly pup,
And the color blue!
Maybe he's *not* the dog for you."

Me? Noisy?
Wait, don't go away...not yet!

I'm a great cuddle-pup with soft blue fuzzle.
Just give me a chance and I'll give you a nuzzle!

Today is the day.
I'll blow them away!

This time my tricks won't fail.
Watch me! I'll catch my crooked tail.

ZOOM-ZOOM-ZOOM!
I can roll over too!

Oops! FLIPPER-FLOP!
My ears made me plop!

Wait...what's that I see?
A squirrel? He's racing me!

"SNORT!" ZOOM! ZOOM!

The big man with the fuzzy face
will tell this man I'm the best.
I think he will be impressed!

"He's a noisy pup,
A messy pup,
A clumsy pup too.
He's a smelly pup,
A silly pup,
And the color blue!
Maybe he's *not* the dog for you."

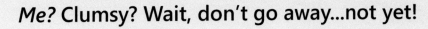

Me? Clumsy? Wait, don't go away...not yet!

Let's play fetch with a ball, or a stick.
Or we can play Frisbee. Take your pick!

Today might be the day.
I hope so anyway.

If only I could see...
I think I hear a family!

"Here we are, my Sweet. What would you like for your
birthday treat?" Daddy says to the little girl.

"I like piglets, pandas, and elephants too.
But I'm not sure which one to choose," she answers.

Mommy shakes her head and says, "Pigs are stinky,
elephants are huge and pandas are quite lazy.
Silly Tilly, do you think we are crazy?"

"How about a giraffe?" Silly Tilly asks.

"A giraffe?" Mommy laughs..."Is much too tall,
how about something that is small?

What you need is a puppy that will run and play and bark.
That's why we came to the Rescue Me Park.
Besides, a giraffe may be as tall as a rocket,
but can you carry one in your pocket?"

Silly Tilly is playing with *every* kind of dog in the Rescue Me Park.

Everyone but *me.*

I'm stuck in the back corner
where I can't be seen.
There must be a way to rescue *me!*

Mommy asks, "Which one do you like, Tilly?
These dogs are all great.
Which one should we pick? It's getting quite late."

"*SNORT!*"

Not yet! I'm over *here!*
Come see *me!* I'm quite near!

Silly Tilly says, "The dogs are nice and friendly too,
but I don't know which one to choose."

Silly Tilly looks sad
and her arms start to flail.
She lets go of her balloon
and lets out a loud wail!

Wait, don't cry.
I can rescue your balloon from the sky.
I'll climb on the fence and jump really high.

YIPPEE! YAHOO! Look at me! I can fly!

BADUMP-BUMP! KER-PLOP!
That landing was quite soft.

I got it! Now don't be sad.
Here's your balloon. Aren't you glad?

Then, at last, she holds me up.
"Look Daddy, I have a blue pup!"

I jump down and around. I laugh with glee!
ZOOM, ZOOM, ZOOM! I am *free!*

I sniff a big stinky shoe.
I stop and begin to chew.

These stringy things sure taste great!
I tug and tug. They move and shake.

The shoe pulls me along.
I pull harder. I am strong!

Now the shoe goes up and down.
And Daddy's falling to the ground.

KABOOM! I *won*! I *won*!
I'm having so much fun!

I lick his face and give a howl.
"*Hooooowwww* do you like me now?"

I want to show them my best dancing move.
Up on two legs, I get in my groove.

Uh-oh, I'm going to fall!
CHOMP! I take a nip, *that's all*.

Mommy says, "Naughty Pup, let go of my dress!
It's brand new. Don't make a mess!"

I shake my head, to and fro.
She pulls me close and won't let go.

YANKETY-YANK! RIPPITY-RIP!
I let go as I tumble and trip.

Then Mommy shakes her dress and stomps her feet,
like a bulldog dancing for a treat!

The big man with the fuzzy face scoops me up
and puts his hands over my ears.
He's talking to my favorite family.
I wish he'd move his hands, so I can hear!

"He's a noisy pup,
A messy pup,
A clumsy pup too.
He's a smelly pup,
A silly pup,
And, he's the color *blue*.
Maybe he's *not* the dog for you?"

Silly Tilly's eyes are big, and her mouth opens wide,
"But he's my favorite color - *blue*!" she cries.

Daddy says softly, "I'm sorry, Tilly, we have to go.
It's time to say 'Adiós'."

"¡Adiós amigo!" She kisses my nose.

She sounds so sad, this *can't* be good-bye.
I've got another trick! I'll give my Spanish a try.

"Good-bye, friend"

"*¡HOLA!*" I bark as loud as I can.

"Wait!" Silly Tilly shouts, "He said hello!
He doesn't want us to go!
He knows Spanish. How can this be?
He knows two languages just like me!"

"A bilingual beagle?" Daddy asks.
"What smiles THAT will bring!
Is there really such a thing?"

Then Mommy says, "Can this really be true?
We speak English and Spanish too!"

The big man with the fuzzy face replies,
"Yep, Yep, he understands both kinds of words,
he's very smart, I'm sure you've heard."

"He's perfect Daddy. He's the pup for me!
Can we take him home? Pretty please?"

"Well...
He's a noisy pup,
A messy pup,
A clumsy pup too.
He's a smelly pup, a silly pup, this could be true.
BUT...
He's smart and determined with a huge heart.
This is the real reason we cannot part.
His snorting and howling are funny, you see.
He most certainly belongs in our family.
This pup is amazing! He's BILINGUAL and BLUE.
I would say, *Woo-hoo Silly Tilly!*
He's the *perfect* pup for you!"

I wriggle and wiggle and waggle my rear.
Then the big man with the fuzzy face whispers in my ear.

"You found a family that sees just how wonderful you are.
They live up the road so you won't be far.
I can let you go now, this was meant to be.
I'm so happy you found your forever-family!"

Mommy asks, "Tilly, what will you call this little blue pup?
Blueberry, Muffin? Peanut Buttercup?"

How silly, I think. I am *not* food.
Does she think she can eat me because I am *blue*?

Silly Tilly giggles and shakes her head *"no."*
Then holds me up as part of the show.

"His name is Ernesto, that's Spanish for Ernie.
But sometimes I'll call him *Ernie-Bo-Bernie*!"

Daddy says, "Ernie the Blue Beagle. That sounds great!
Now let's take him home and celebrate."

He carefully tucks me into Silly Tilly's pouch,
I'm cozy and warm as I curl up and slouch.

I look back at my friends and let out a loud bark.
I'm so glad we met at the Rescue Me Park!

The pet store clerk told me Ernie would never be a show dog. He was blue, the runt of the litter, had crooked teeth, his tail was bent, and he really did snort just like a little piglet. I thought he was perfect exactly the way he was and I adopted him right away!

Ernie learned his commands in Spanish and English and at just 9 weeks old, understood both languages. I realized early on that he was one special pup! Not only was he a blue beagle, he was also bilingual!

People were drawn to Ernie because he was unique and frequently inquired about his coloring. I was often asked if he was a pure beagle because he looked so different. Ernie was smart, funny, ornery at times but very charming. He had a way of making everyone smile and laugh.

Sadly Ernie passed away just two months shy of his 15th birthday, but my hope is that his legacy will live on and children will learn many of the life lessons Ernie taught me. Perhaps the most profound lesson of all, is to embrace our uniqueness and not be afraid to stand out.

"In a pack of beagles, always be an Ernie!"

- Sarah Tooker